The Thirsty Moose is based
on a traditional Native
American story

This edition published 2009, by Zero to Ten Limited,
part of the Evans Publishing Group
2A Portman Mansions
Chiltern St
London W1U 6NR

Text copyright © Evans Brothers Ltd 2004
© in the illustrations Mike Gordon 2004

British Library Cataloguing in Publication Data
A CIP catalogue record for this book Is available from the British
Library

ISBN: 9781840895728

Printed in Hong Kong by New Era Co. Ltd

The Thirsty Moose

by David Orme

illustrated by Mike Gordon

ZERO TO TEN

Big Moose was thirsty.

He went to the river and
drank and drank.

The water went down
and down.

"Stop it!" shouted the beaver.
"My home will be spoiled!"

But Big Moose wouldn't listen.

"Stop it!" shouted the muskrat.
"I'll have nowhere to swim!"

Big Moose still
wouldn't listen.

"Stop it!" bubbled the fish. "We can't live without water!"

Big Moose still wouldn't listen.

"Stop it!" buzzed the fly.
"Or I'll fight you!"

Big Moose listened this time.

"Go on," said Big Moose.
"I dare you!"

Big Moose started
drinking again.

The fly flew into Big Moose's ear.

"I'll teach you not to listen!" he buzzed. Then he started to bite.

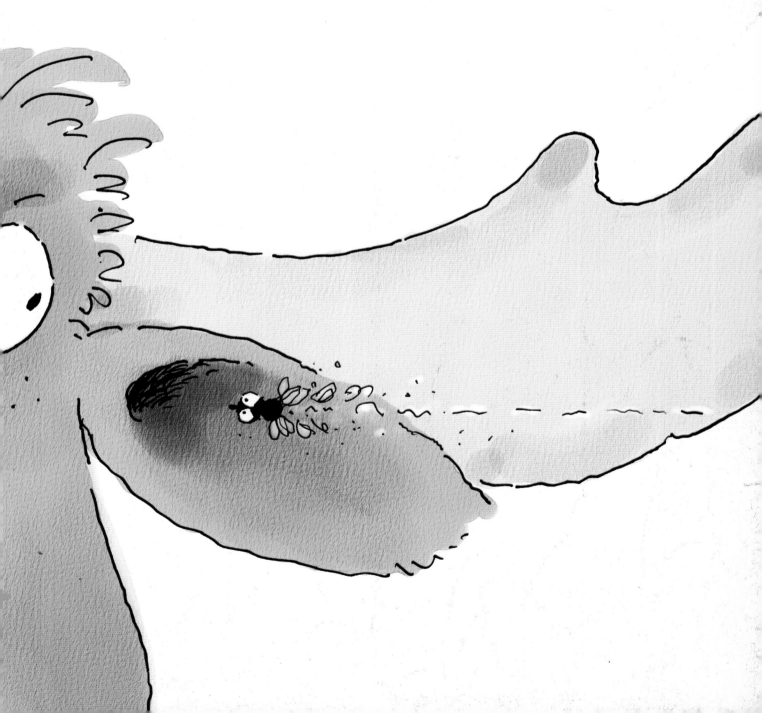

"Stop it!" shouted Big Moose.

But the fly didn't stop.
Big Moose ran away
as fast as he could.

He never came back
to the river again!